NOTHING EVER HAPPENS ON MY BLOCK

ELLEN RASKIN

NOTHING
ever happens
on MY BLOCK

ATHENEUM, New York, 1971

Library of Congress catalog card number 66-12853
Published simultaneously in Canada by McClelland & Stewart Ltd.
Manufactured in the United States of America
Printed by Connecticut Printers, Hartford
Bound by H. Wolff, New York
First Printing February 1966
Ninth Printing June 1971

This book is dedicated
to Susan,
Patty, Steve and Larry,
Mike and Helene, Nelle, Gina
and children everywhere,
except Chester Filbert.
He's just too dull.

My name is Chester Filbert.

I live at 5264 West One hundred and seventy-seventh Street.

Some places have marching bands

or haunted houses,

courageous hunters hunting

ferocious lions and tigers,

pirates and buried treasure,

Indians on the warpath,

deep-sea divers,

monsters, astronauts, spies licensed to kill, unclimbed mountains to climb

even fireworks.

But nothing ever happens on my block.

When I grow up I'm going to move.